THE
BLABBERMOUTHS

Adapted from a German Folktale

by Gerda Mantinband
pictures by Paul Borovsky

Greenwillow Books New York

For Laurel
—G. M.

For my brother, Jakub
—P. B.

Watercolors, colored pencils, and a black pen
were used for the full-color art.
The text type is Schneidler Medium.
Text copyright © 1992 by Gerda B. Mantinband
Illustrations copyright © 1992 by Paul Borovsky
All rights reserved. No part of this book
may be reproduced or utilized in any form
or by any means, electronic or mechanical,
including photocopying, recording, or by
any information storage and retrieval
system, without permission in writing
from the Publisher, Greenwillow Books,
a division of William Morrow & Company, Inc.,
1350 Avenue of the Americas, New York, NY 10019.
Printed in Singapore by Tien Wah Press
First Edition   10 9 8 7 6 5 4 3 2 1

Library of Congress Cataloging-in-Publication Data

Mantinband, Gerda.
The blabbermouths / by Gerda Mantinband;
pictures by Paul Borovsky.
p.   cm.
Summary: Although he swears not to reveal the
source of his new-found wealth, a poor farmer
can't help telling his wife and then a neighbor,
and soon the news is all over town.
ISBN 0-688-10602-1 (trade).
ISBN 0-688-10604-8 (lib.)
[1. Gossip—Fiction.]   I. Title.
PZ7.M3184B1   1992
[E]—dc20   91-30062   CIP   AC

Once upon a time a poor farmer drove his horse and cart to the forest to cut some wood. At the edge of the forest stood a mighty oak tree, and under it, in the mist, an old woman sat huddled by an iron chest.

She called out to him. The farmer was a timid man and would have driven past her, but when he heard what she had to say, he stopped.

"I'm under a spell," she said. "You can set me free and do yourself some good into the bargain."

He could hardly believe it when she added, "How would you like to take this chest home with you? It's chock-full of gold pieces."

"I'd like that very well!" said the astounded farmer.

"But there's one condition," the old woman replied. "You must not breathe a word of this to a living soul."

"Why would I?" the farmer said indignantly. "Do you think I am a blabbermouth?"

The old woman helped the farmer drag
the heavy chest onto his cart and, lickety-
split and clippety-clop, he drove back to
his village.

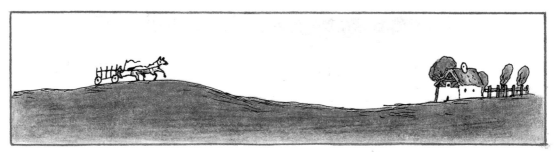

He had hardly got through his farmyard gate
when he shouted, "Wife! Wife! You'll never guess
what I've got here." And in a lower voice he
added, "I'm not to tell a living soul, but you're
my wife. See this chest? It's chock-full of gold
pieces."

"Never," said the woman, clapping her hands
to her cheeks in amazement.

"We'll not be poor again," the farmer said
proudly. "Let's cook a feast. We haven't tasted
meat in many a day."

The woman helped her husband drag
the chest into the cellar. He gave her a gold
piece, and she went shopping. Soon after
she returned, the most delicious smells
drifted from her kitchen.

Before long their neighbor came sniffing at the door. "What good things do you have cooking in your pot?" she asked.

The farmer was bursting with his good news. "Oh, neighbor," he said. "Can you keep a secret?"

"Of course," the neighbor said indignantly. "Do you think I'm a blabbermouth?"

"Certainly not," said the farmer. "That's why I can tell it to you. But make sure not to breathe a word of this to a living soul! What do you think I found in the woods this morning?"

"What?" asked the neighbor, her eyes bulging with curiosity.

"An iron chest chock-full of gold pieces, that's what!"

"What luck!" said the neighbor, and clapped her hands in wonder. "It's a good thing you've not told anyone else. People are so jealous. But now I must run."

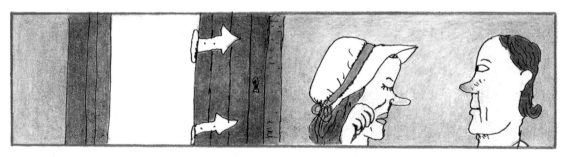

She hurried away, but she didn't go home.
As fast as she could, she ran to her brother's
house and cried, "Would you believe it! The
farmer across the road found a chest chock-
full of gold pieces in the woods this morning.
But mind you don't tell anyone!"

"Of course not," said her brother and his
wife. "Do we look like blabbermouths?"

And so the news got to the butcher,
the baker, the candlestick maker, and
everyone else who lived in the village.
Before long it reached the ears of the
magistrate.

He sent for the farmer, but the farmer
was too shy to go and sent his wife instead.
"Don't bother to deny it," the magistrate
thundered. "Your husband stole a chest
chock-full of gold pieces. Just hand the
money over."

"Oh, that's not true," the farmer's wife said. "He's as poor as a church mouse and as honest as the day is long. He hasn't stolen anything."

"Not so," said the magistrate. "He himself told the tale."

"And a tale it was!" laughed the farmer's wife. "Don't listen to him. He's crazy."

"We'll soon see," said the magistrate. "You be here in two weeks when the court meets."

When she got home, the farmer was in the barn, and his wife went quietly into the cellar, took a gold piece from the chest, and drove back into town. She stopped at both bakeries and bought as many doughnuts as they had.

When she returned home, she made sure that her husband was still in the barn. She scattered doughnuts all around, put a few by the gate, and threw some on the roof.

Then she went to the barn and cried, "Husband! Come and see what has happened! The Good Lord let it rain doughnuts!"

"Rain doughnuts?" he asked. "Are you crazy?"

"Look for yourself if you don't believe me," said his wife.

The farmer ran out to the yard and
was overjoyed when he found doughnuts scattered everywhere. He picked
up every one, and when he was done,
there was a barrel-full.

A few days later, the farmer's wife said,
"Listen, husband. I'm scared to death. I just
heard that the king has hired soldiers from far
away. They have long, pointed, iron beaks with
which they stab to death anyone they find.
They're supposed to pass through our village
today. They must not find us. Why don't you
hide under the big washtub, and I'll hide in the
attic? When they see there is no one at home,
they'll leave."

The timid farmer was glad to help his wife roll the big, heavy washtub into the nearby meadow. The farmer turned it over and crawled under it.

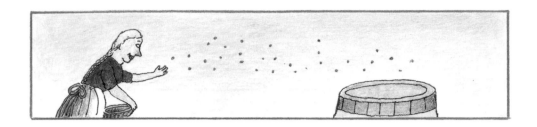

"Keep very quiet," his wife warned. Then she got a sack of corn from the barn, scattered some on the washtub, and let the chickens out of their coop.

They ran around pecking at the corn—pick, pick, pick, and peck, peck, peck—until it was all gone. Then they ran back into the farmyard.

Soon the farmer's wife knocked on the washtub and said, "You can come out now. The soldiers are gone. Thank goodness we're safe. They didn't find me, either."

The farmer said, "I surely was scared. When they went pick, pick, pick on the washtub, I thought my last hour had come."

When the two weeks had gone by, the farmer
and his wife went to court. The farmer denied
everything. No, no, he had stolen nothing. He
swore that everything had happened just as he
had told his neighbor.

"When was it, dear, that you brought the
money home?" asked the wife.

"Don't you remember?" cried the husband.
"It was just two days before the Good Lord let
it rain doughnuts."

The magistrate and the jurors looked
at one another and shook their heads.
"And then the king's soldiers came
and with their long, iron beaks went
pick, pick, pick on the washtub."

Everybody shook their heads again. "He's
mad," they whispered to one another, and
to the farmer's wife the magistrate said,

"You're right, he does tell tales. Now,
go home and don't let him make any
more mischief."

So the farmer and his wife went
home, and they lived happily ever after.